T0145279

Live;
Love;
Laugh;
Pray

Written by:
Pricilla Hopkins
2/17/09

To order additional copies of this book, contact:
Xlibris
844-714-8691
www.Xlibris.com
Orders@Xlibris.com

ISBN: Softcover   978-1-4415-3359-3
        EBook   978-1-6698-5558-3

Print information available on the last page

Rev. date: 11/10/2022

One upon a time there was a little girl named known as Naomi Kim born with a holy gift, which were psychic powers.

At two, she could detect and predict when something phenomenally perverse was going to happen to some one.

When she was starting out in the kindergarten at five the nursery, bus would drop her off at brewer-Benton nursery school.

One day she was taking her 2-hour nap before the bus was to return to take her back home.

She saw the bus turn over in her mind and screamed and called staff; staff; staff.

Please do not make me get on that bus today. And they wondered why she said that.

In addition, the bus was late and never came to get her because it skidded on slick ice pavement and went over the rail on the expressway.

Therefore, they called her mother miss Naomi Kim Sr. to pick her up and told them that her daughter had predicted that the bus would crash ant that she had said, so please do not make me get on it to go back home.

Therefore, her mother started thinking about her grandfather from when he was her age that his brother was going to be killed by a British regime and wired Great Britain about getting him onto that plane.

That evening, and said that bus was late and never came to get her because it sledded on slick pavement, and went over the rail of the expressway. so they called her mother Miss Naomi-Kim Sr. to pick her up and told them that her daughter had predicted that the bus would crash and she said please don't make be get on it to go back home.

Therefore, her mother started thinking about her grandfather from when he was her age, that his brother was going to be killed by a British regime and wired Great Britain about getting him not to get that plane that evening.

In addition, save his brother from being killed that day.

In addition, up to this day, his brother lived to be a 110 years old.

One day again Naomi-Kim say her mother in her mind kissing her good-bye for the last time and getting into a New York taxi cab, and held at gun point for money, and jewelry.

Therefore, she told her mother about the dream.

Instead of her mother catching the cab taxi at seven o'clock in the morning her mother listen to Naomi-Kim Jr. and did not take the taxi to work that morning.

Because of her psychic-gift, Naomi-Kim was removed from her home at 9 years old and is now a psychic nun in Bei-ginh China.

Discovering medicine, and formulas for people to drink and eat to live to be past the age of her grandfathers brother, of which whom lived to be a young but healthy young up to 110 years old.

A Proverb: confusions say think before you act, do, and say.

The End

Priscilla and her son Shelton at age 1 with Shelton's friend Bryan Edmondson

Shelton celebrating Easter

Shelton begging me not to snap has his picture taken

Priscilla teaching Shelton his first step

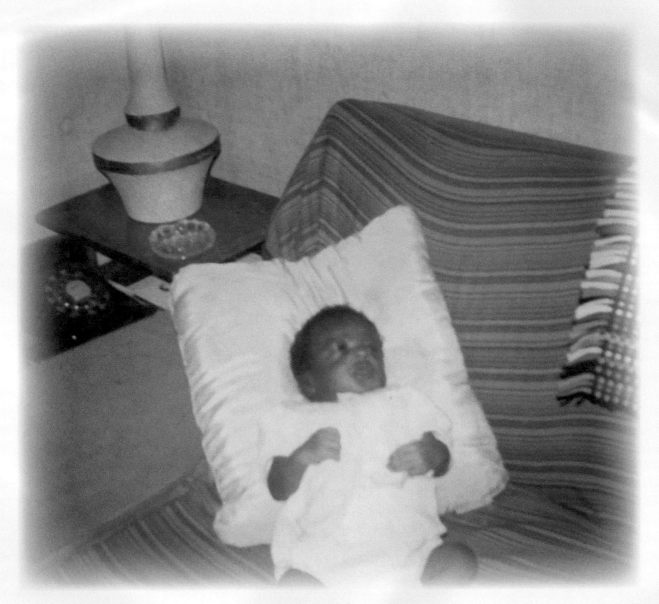

Shelton at 2 days old

My Wedding

Mr. and Mrs. Thearthur Hopkins Jr. and Priscilla June Peters

My Wedding

My Nephews Adam and Isaac Peters

Wedding pictures of
Pierre Hopkins and Lacresha Ann Hopkins

My daughter- in- law Lacresha Ann Hopkins

My Grandson - Jaleel Friday

*My daughter- in- law Lacresha Ann Hopkins
and my granddaughter Jasmin age 8
and my Niece Kokamoe age 4*

*My Son Pierre Hopkins and The Bride, Lacresha Ann
and my ex-husband Thearthur Hopkins Jr.*

My Best Friend and my favorite mailman

Lonnie

In loving memory of...

*Shelton's Favorite Uncle Alvin and guardian angel
who was more of a father to him than anyone else
and will be well remembered.*

Henry Louis Watson
July 7, 1946- August 29, 2007

A Best Friend to be remembered ~ Priscilla

My name is Priscilla Hopkins. I was born on June 2, 1954. My mother and father's name is Mrs. Laveda and James Peters. My mother is an 86 year old deaconess. My best friend in the world is my new friend Mr. Steven Mason. He works at J&J Appliances in Tulsa, OK on 21st in Garnet St. He usually helps me financially when I need food or medication. He comes from a Christian Family. My Auntie's name is Sannie Whitney. She is like a mother to me and my other friend is a Christian woman by the name of Harriet Hampton she is my best friend also. I graduated from Booker T. WA senior high school in 1972.

My book deals with a little girl with psychic powers. You will enjoy my book because it is a tear jerker. My book also reflects how smart children are. When you read my book, you will realize that kids also have a holy gift. Kids can help you with so many things if you teach them about God while they are young.

I, Priscilla Hopkins worked at a church nursery and deal with kids.